D0478925

Rabén & Sjögren Stockholm


Originally published in 1991 by Rabén & Sjögren under the title

Library of Congress catalog card number: 91-40847
Printed in Italy
First edition, 1993

ISBN 91 29 62064 3

Astrid Lindgren

# The Day Adam Got Mad

Pictures by Marit Törnqvist

*Translated by Barbara Lucas*

R&S BOOKS

Stockholm New York London Adelaide Toronto

This is the story of the great bull, Adam, who got loose on an Easter day a long time ago. He might still be loose if only — well, here's what happened.

Adam was a huge bull. He lived in a barn in Sweden together with rows of round cows and many sweet calves. Actually, Adam was a kind and good-natured bull. The farmhand who fed the animals in the barn was also kind and good-natured. Svensson was his name, and he was so kind that one time when Adam accidentally stepped on Svensson's foot Svensson didn't have the heart to push him aside. He just stood there quietly until Adam himself decided to move.

So why should a bull suddenly become so angry? Why did Adam get into such a dangerous mood on that particular day? We may never know. Perhaps one of the calves said something rude to him in calf talk, or perhaps the cows teased him. In any case, right in the middle of that Easter morning, Adam broke loose and came thundering down the length of the barn with such a terrible look that Svensson decided not to stand there and ask what was the matter. Svensson ran for his life out the barn door. And Adam came after him in a wild rage.

Outside the barn was the barnyard, surrounded by a fence. Svensson managed to bolt through the gate and shut it right on Adam's nose as he prepared to run his horns through his old friend.

It was, as you know, Easter day, and inside the farmhouse sat the farmer and his family eating their breakfast in peace and quiet. It was a beautiful day and the children in the house were happy, not so much because they were going to church, but because they were going to wear their new sandals, and because the sun was shining so nicely, and because in the afternoon they planned to play at the creek by the meadow filled with anemones.

But that never happened. Nothing happened, because of Adam.

Down in the barnyard he rushed back and forth bellowing madly. Svensson stood on the other side of the fence, looking helplessly at him, trembling with fright. Soon, everyone was gathered there — the farmer and the children, the servants and the farmhands — all watching the raging animal. By then, the news had spread throughout the countryside: a prize bull was running around like a roaring lion in the barnyard.

From all the houses and cottages for miles around, people came, eager to watch this drama. They were all exhilarated to have a little excitement interrupting a long, quiet Easter day.

Karl from the neighboring town was one of the first to come running, as fast as his small, seven-year-old-boy legs could carry him. He was a little Swedish farm boy, exactly like a thousand others — blue-eyed, flaxen-haired, runny-nosed.

Adam had been loose for two hours now, and so far, no one could figure out how to get him to calm down and come to his senses. The farmer decided to try to get nearer. He went inside the fenced-in barnyard and took several determined steps toward the bull. He never should have done that! Adam had decided to be angry on this Easter day and was going to stay that way. He lowered his head and rushed at the farmer, and if the farmer had not jumped away, who knows how it might have ended. As it was, there was only a great big tear in his nice churchgoing trousers, which happened as he made his hasty escape through the barnyard gate. The spectators looked at one another and smiled quietly.

What a foolish situation!

In the barn, the cows began to moo. It was time for their midday milking. But who would dare cross the barnyard to get into the barn? No one!

"What if Adam decides to be mad forever, as long as we live!" said one small child. That was a sad thought. How, then, could they play hide-and-seek in the barn on winter evenings?

Easter day stretched on: the sun shone, and Adam was angry. On the other side of the fence, there were anxious discussions. If someone could get near the animal with a long pole, perhaps that person could hook it into his nose ring? Or would they be forced to shoot him, crazy as he was? Certainly *this* couldn't be allowed to continue. In the barn, the cows bellowed, their udders tightening.

The sun was shining, the sky was blue, the birch trees had put out their first ruffling leaves. Everything was as lovely as it could possibly be on an Easter day in Sweden. But Adam was angry.

Perched up on the fence was Karl, a little runny-nosed farm boy, barely seven years old.

"Adam," he said. "Come over here and I'll scratch you right between your horns." Even if Adam understood him, he didn't pay any attention. Not to begin with, anyway. Because he was angry. But that tender little voice said, over and over again, "Come over here, and I'll scratch you right between your horns."

Perhaps, in the end, it turned out not to be as much fun to be angry as Adam had thought. He began to hesitate. And as he hesitated, he came closer to the fence where Karl was sitting. Karl scratched him between the horns with his small dirty farm-boy fingers, all the while prattling on in his friendly manner.

Adam seemed a little embarrassed to be standing still, letting his head be scratched. But still he stood. Then Karl took a firm grip on Adam's nose ring and climbed over the fence.

"Have you lost your mind, child?" somebody shouted.

Slowly and carefully, Karl led Adam by his nose ring right up to the barn door. Adam was a big, big bull, and Karl was a small, small boy. They made rather a sweet pair as they walked across the barnyard.

A Spanish matador could not have received greater applause than Karl did when he returned from the barn after leading Adam to his stall. Yes, applause, and two crowns, and a dozen eggs in a bag were the young bullfighter's reward.

"I'm used to animals, you see," explained Karl. "I talk to them all the time."

Then he turned on his heel and went back home with two crowns in his pocket and a bag of eggs in his hand, quite satisfied with his Easter day.

And there he goes, a Swedish bullfighter amid the pale, pale green birch trees.